Dedicated in loving memory to Paul Staller.

My name is **MOE.** I'm a turtle and I live with
my mom in a small house on the beach.
I'm tiny. Really tiny. And I can play the guitar too.
Sometimes it's hard to hold a musical instrument
in my little flippers.

I also love to read. But what I really want to do
is write **BOOKS!**

It all began on the last day of **SUMMER** when my mom was walking with me on the beach to dig in the sand for shells. It was getting chilly outside.

No one was **SWIMMING,** but I noticed a little girl with a big bow on top of her curly golden hair. She was leaning down collecting pretty shells and dropping them into her big pink bucket.

She couldn't see me because I'm so SMALL.
I watched her for a long time and forgot it was
getting late. When I looked up for my mom,
she was gone!

Then I heard my mom calling my name.
I ran to catch up with her as
fast as my LITTLE FLIPPERS could carry me.

Remember, I told you I'm very small. It's not easy being so little and I tend to get left behind quite a lot. You should have guessed by now that I'm not one of those big Galapagos tortoises or even a mean **SNAPPER** turtle.

In fact, I'm so teeny I bet I could sit on the tip of your thumb. I'm a little forgetful sometimes but I'm **NEVER** ever mean. When I get scared, I quickly poke my head back inside my shell and hide.
Like **RIGHT NOW!**

The little girl is coming towards me. Oh no! I'm afraid she is going to step on me. I'll use my flippers to dig a hole in the sand so I can hide.

It worked! She passed right by me.
Phew, that was close. The next morning when I
woke up, I remembered it was the first day
of school. Mom called out to me,
"Moe! Finish your breakfast. You don't want to
be late for school. Brush your shell, wash your
FLIPPERS and don't forget to wear your jacket.
Now let me give you a big **KISS.**"
"**YUCK, MOM!** I have to get going."

"Now Moe, go straight to **SCHOOL.**
No wandering off to the beach today."
As I left the house, I yelled
"Bye mom...I am going to make some
NEW FRIENDS today!"
I wanted to bring a present for my teacher.
I remembered those pretty shells that I saw on
the beach... it would only take a minute.

After all, school was very **CLOSE,**
just one sand dune away.
I still had plenty of time before school began.
As I reached the water, I saw that same
little girl again. Maybe she was **PICKING** shells
for her teacher too!

She was coming closer and almost **STEPPED** on me. Suddenly, I felt myself lifted up into the air and **DROPPED** into her pink bucket. Oh no!

She didn't realize she had
grabbed **ME** along with the other shells.
I yelled, "HELP! What's **HAPPENING?**"
I was tossed around and around in her bucket.
Where was she taking me?

The ride was so bumpy that I **FLIPPED** over and landed upside down. The little girl's hand reached down to **PICK OUT** some shells. One by one, **SHELLS** disappeared all around me. Then, without warning, I felt myself lifted into the air.

"Oh my, what is this? It's not a shell,
it's a **TURTLE!**" said the little girl.

"Hi there little fella. What's your name?"
"M-m-m-my name is Moe," I squeaked.
"Wow a **TALKING** turtle! Nice to meet you, Moe.
My name is Molly. What are you doing in my
bucket?" she asked with a **BIG SMILE.**

I tried to speak in my **LOUDEST** voice.
"I don't know. What happened, Molly? Where am I?
Where is the turtle classroom?"
"I'm sorry I don't know.
You're in **MY** classroom now" she said.
"Would you like to **SEE** it?"

Compared to my tiny house on the **SAND DUNE,** the school seemed so big. The room was filled with desks and chairs. The walls were painted **BLUE** and **PURPLE** and covered with children's drawings.
I could hear the children playing and laughing while they hung up their jackets getting ready for the school day.

Meanwhile, Molly held me in her hand
while the other children rushed around to find
their desks. "Moe, would you like to see my
FAVORITE corner of the room?"

Suddenly, a little boy bumped into Molly and she dropped
me on the floor. Oh no! I was upside down again.
Molly bent down and gently scooped me up into her hands.
"Thank you, Molly. Next time I promise to HOLD on to
your thumb with my FLIPPERS as tightly as I can."

"Moe, before class begins let's
walk over to the book corner."
"BOOKS! REALLY? I LOVE BOOKS!
I'm going to be a writer someday." I said.
"Wow, Moe. A turtle who not only talks, but writes
too! But how are you going to hold a pen
with your flippers? Would you like me to HELP you?"
"Yes! Thanks, Molly."
Molly and I sat down on a big, comfy chair
and read books together.
We almost forgot to stop and eat lunch!

I found a book about turtles. There were big ones, small ones and even tiny turtles like me. I had so much **FUN** reading that day in Molly's classroom that I never wanted to leave.

Molly looked at the clock. "It's getting late. We'll have to find your class tomorrow." When the closing bell **RANG,** I was tired and ready to go home to tell mom about my new friend, Molly.

After school Molly walked me home to the beach where she had found me that morning. Before she left she **PROMISED** to pick me up the next day and walk to school with me.

My mom was waiting for me when I got home.
"Moe, how was your first day of school?" she asked.
"MOM! I made a new **FRIEND!**
And there were so many books to read. I even found
books about turtles like me!
I can't **WAIT** to go back **TOMORROW.**"

THE END

DID YOU KNOW?

There are at least 365 species of turtles and tortoises in the world. But what are the differences between turtles and tortoises anyway? The biggest difference is where they live. Turtles spend most of their time in the ocean or near water while tortoises live on land.

Tortoises can live very long lives. The oldest one living is said to be a Seychelles giant tortoise named Jonathan, who is turning 190 years old in 2022.

A Galapagos tortoise named Harriet was discovered by Charles Darwin in 1835. She died in 2006, having lived for approximately 176 years.

(Wikipedia 2022)

Paul Staller graduated from Stockton University in 1997
and University of Pittsburgh Law School in 2002.
He passed away too soon in 2014.

Paul left behind volumes of sketches, drawings and writings.
Moe the Turtle is a character we found in one of his notebooks.

This book was inspired by those drawings.

Proceeds from Little Moe to be donated to the
Stockton University Writing Center.